Black Beauty

adapted by Carol Joan Drexler

illustrated by Norman Nodel

Educational Reading Service

MAHWAH, NEW JERSEY

© Educational Reading Service, 1970
Library of Congress Catalog Card No. 73-121129
Copyright © 1970, Shelley Graphics, Ltd., U.K.

Black Beauty was a very handsome young horse. He was black all over, except for a white star on his forehead.

He was owned by a good man named Squire Gordon, who kept several horses. Black Beauty's special friends were a little fat pony named Merrylegs, and a tall chestnut mare named Ginger. The three of them loved to run and play together in the fields.

Squire Gordon and his wife and children took good care of their horses, and they loved to go riding out in their carriage with John Manly, the groom, carefully driving Black Beauty and Ginger.

One day Squire Gordon had to go to town on business, even though the weather was very bad. The roads were full of deep puddles, and the branches of the trees overhead hung low from the weight of their wet leaves.

John Manly drove Black Beauty very carefully, so he wouldn't stumble. When they got to town, Squire Gordon went about his business, while John saw to it that Black Beauty had a good lunch while they waited.

By the time the Squire was ready to go home, it was raining even harder than before.

When they got to the bridge, it was pitch dark and their carriage lantern did very little to light their way in the storm.

In the middle of the bridge, Black Beauty suddenly stopped dead and refused to go another step. "What is it, my beauty?" John called out. "Go on, boy. Get us home and out of this storm!"

But Black Beauty wouldn't budge. When John took the lantern off the carriage and walked a few steps forward, he saw why his good horse had disobeyed him — part of the bridge had been washed away by the flooding river racing below it!

"Black Beauty has saved our lives!" John called back to the Squire. By the pale light of the lantern, they could see that one more step would have meant their deaths. Deeply grateful to their good horse, they turned the carriage around and went home another way.

One day not too long after, the Squire came running down to the stable, calling out, "John, John! Rush as quickly as you can to the doctor in the village, and tell him to come at once! Mrs. Gordon is desperately ill!"

John saddled Black Beauty, and the two of them raced off into the night, galloping the long eight miles to town just as fast as they could go.

When they got to the doctor's house, John shouted until the shutters were thrown open. When the doctor finally understood what was the matter, he called down, "I would gladly come at once, but my horse is lame, and I have no other. What shall I do?"

John called back, "Black Beauty is tired, but I'm sure he will carry you as fast as he carried me. I feel he knows what is happening, and wants to help in his own way."

And John was right, for though he was very tired from his long run, Black Beauty took the doctor back to Squire Gordon's even faster than he had come.

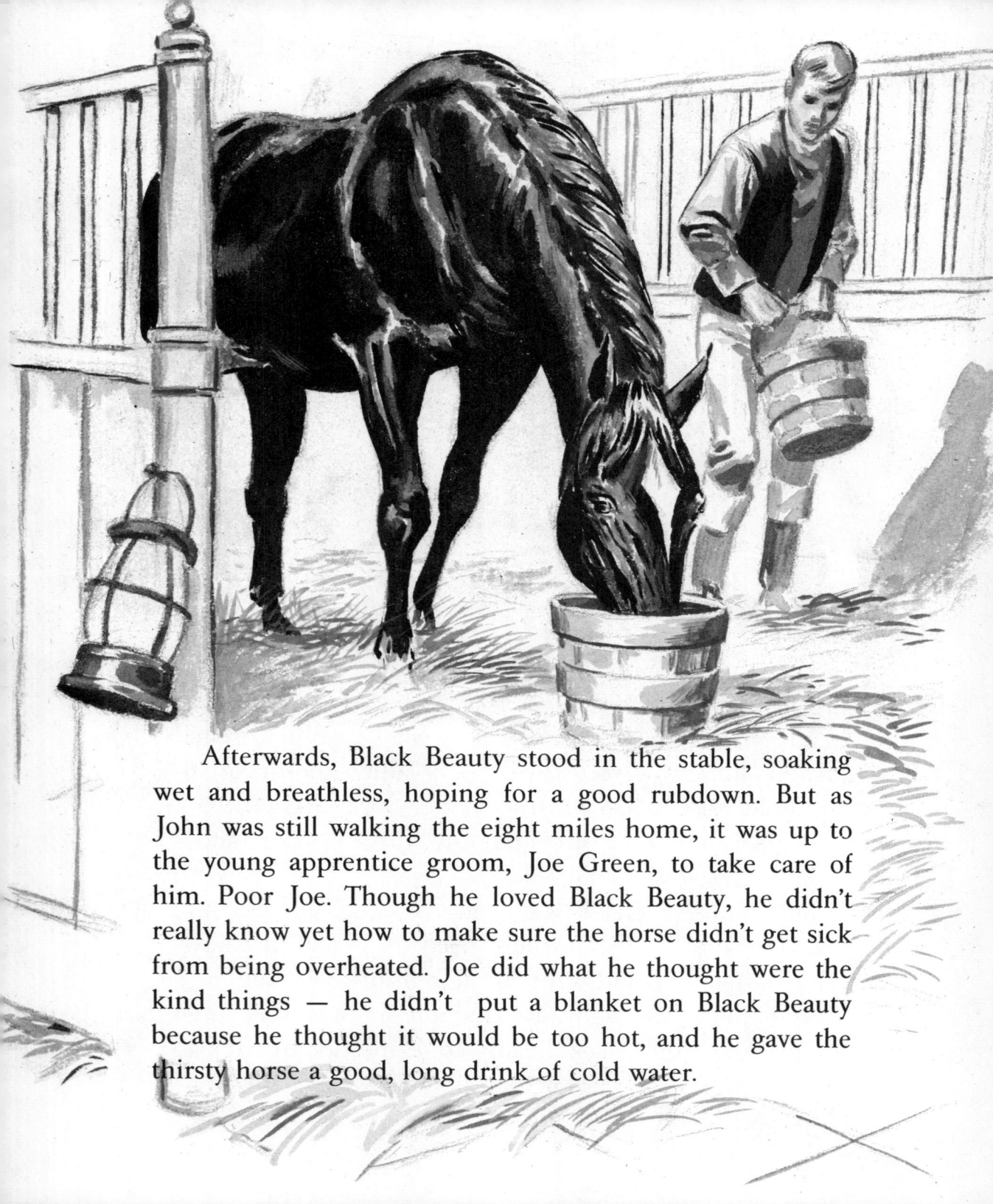

Afterwards, Black Beauty stood in the stable, soaking wet and breathless, hoping for a good rubdown. But as John was still walking the eight miles home, it was up to the young apprentice groom, Joe Green, to take care of him. Poor Joe. Though he loved Black Beauty, he didn't really know yet how to make sure the horse didn't get sick from being overheated. Joe did what he thought were the kind things — he didn't put a blanket on Black Beauty because he thought it would be too hot, and he gave the thirsty horse a good, long drink of cold water.

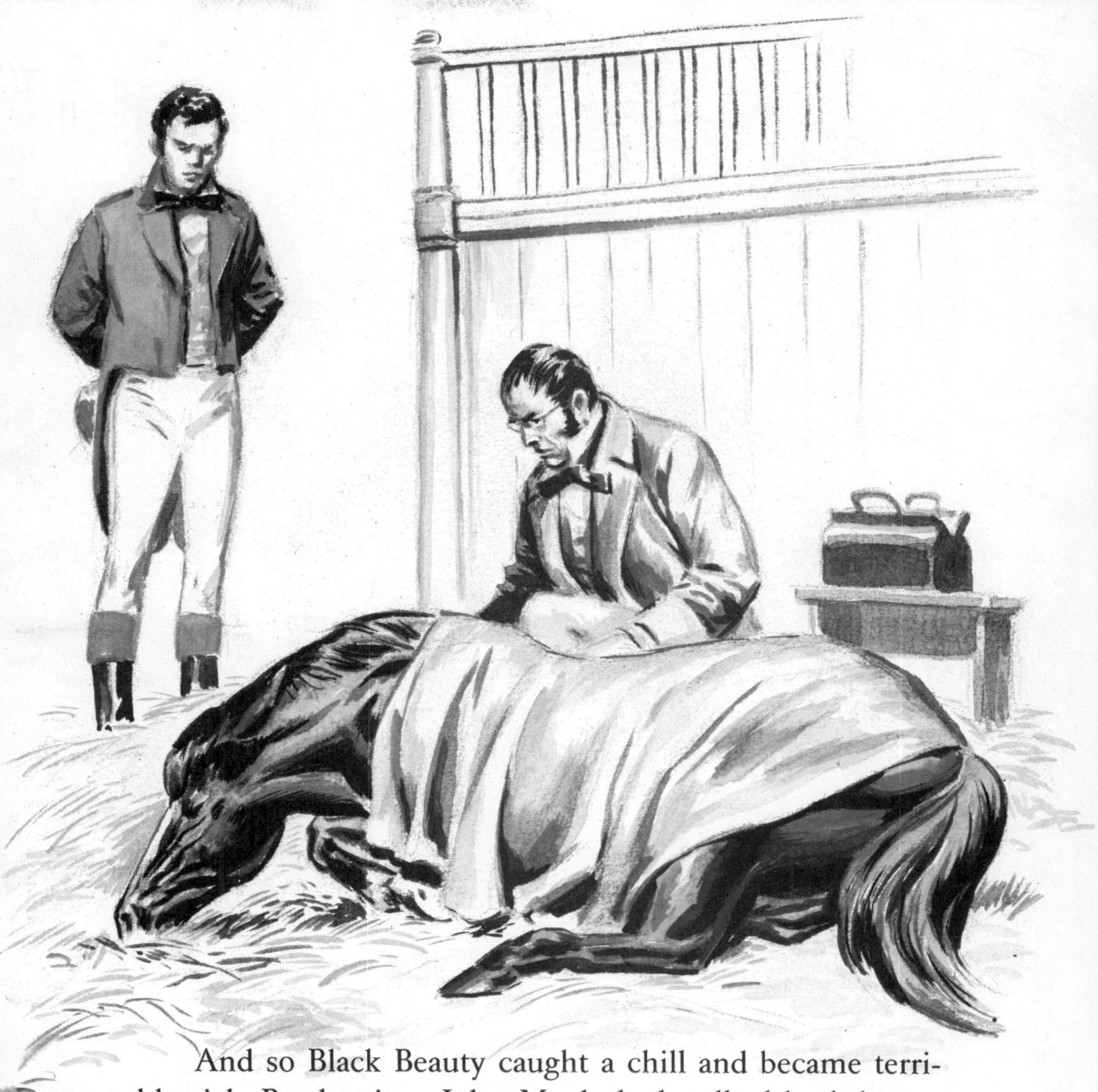

And so Black Beauty caught a chill and became terribly sick. By the time John Manly had walked back home, Black Beauty was trembling with chills and a fever. John ran for the horse doctor, and he and the doctor stayed with Black Beauty through that first bad night, until he was out of danger.

After many weeks, Black Beauty was finally well again — but Squire Gordon's wife was still sick. "If your wife is to live, you must move to a warmer climate," the doctor told Squire Gordon. And the Squire came down to the stable to talk to John. "I'm afraid we're going to have to close the house and sell the horses, John," he said. "I'll see that you and Joe have good jobs before we leave. I wish there was another way — we shall miss you all very much..."

Ginger and Merrylegs were sold very quickly at the horse fair. They bade a sad goodbye to their friend. Then Black Beauty saw a very pleasant and cheerful-looking man watching him. The man looked Black Beauty over very carefully. He gently stroked the horse's body, checked his teeth, and walked around him, talking softly, like a friend. Black Beauty hoped the man would buy him — and he did.

Black Beauty's new owner was Jeremiah Barker — Jerry for short — and he lived in London and drove a hansom cab there.

As they drove into his stableyard that night, Jerry called out, "Ho! Polly, Harry, Dolly, come see the newest member of our family!" In a second, Jerry's wife and children came running out of the house eager to meet their new horse.

The next morning, Black Beauty began his new job of pulling Jerry's cab through the crowded streets of London. Jerry was a wonderful and careful driver, and he and Black Beauty made a good team for getting in and out of the tight squeezes of city traffic.

One evening, a customer kept Jerry and Black Beauty waiting many hours in a freezing rainstorm. Jerry walked up and down, stamping his feet and trying to keep warm. Black Beauty stood there feeling his own legs getting stiff with the cold.

When they finally got home that night, Jerry was coughing badly and was very sick. Harry came out to the stable and took care of Black Beauty, while his mother put Jerry to bed and called the doctor.

Harry and Dolly came every day for the next few weeks to take care of Black Beauty — but Jerry never came again.

"Oh, Black Beauty, Dad is so sick we'll have to leave London," Dolly said, as she combed him one morning. And Harry added, "The doctor says he must never drive a cab again. He must work at an easier job from now on. And we're going to have to leave you behind!" Then both children burst into tears and ran out of the stable.

A few days later, a weeping Polly took Black Beauty to the horse fair, and there he was sold to a baker.

The baker was a mean man, and he made Black Beauty carry loads that were much too heavy. When Black Beauty couldn't pull the wagon, the baker thought he was lazy, and sold him to a wicked man who owned many cabs and who abused all his horses. Black Beauty was so overworked and underfed that he soon became too weak to work. So the cab owner decided to sell him — and this time Black Beauty's luck changed. As he stood at the horse fair, his head drooping and his ribs showing right through his skin, Black Beauty heard a young boy say, "Oh, grandfather! This horse must have been really handsome once. I just know he's been mistreated. Grandfather, we could make him well again. See how gentle his eyes

are, and how he looks at us? Oh, grandfather, please buy him!"

And so Black Beauty was bought by farmer Thoroughgood who, with his grandson, set out to make their new horse well again.

After months of resting in the good farmer's pasture, and being tended by the young grandson, Black Beauty looked and acted like his old self. He pranced and galloped and played in the field, and ate his food with a good appetite. The boy groomed him every day, and his coat became sleek and shiny once again.

One day a young man came to look over the horses farmer Thoroughgood had for sale. As he came into the stable he exclaimed, "Why, this horse looks just like a horse I used to know when I was a boy. That white star on his forehead — it's Black Beauty! Do you remember me, boy? I'm Joe Green — all grown up and a lot smarter about horses!"

Black Beauty nickered happily, and Joe Green patted him and told the farmer he wanted to buy the beautiful black horse. The farmer's grandson was sad, but he knew Black Beauty would have a good home and the best of care.

And so Black Beauty went to live with Joe Green and the two ladies Joe worked for. Several times a week they would all go for a drive in the fresh air, and in between times, Black Beauty would be allowed to rest or play in the pasture, and to eat his good food and enjoy having Joe take care of him.

Black Beauty had found another good home and another fine master. Though he still missed Squire Gordon, and John Manly, and Jerry Barker — Black Beauty was happy once again.